PUP IN SCHOOL

ELAINE CLAYTON

CROWN PUBLISHERS INC. *New York*

For my mom and dad
and brothers and sisters

Published by Crown Publishers, Inc., a Random House company,
225 Park Avenue South, New York, New York 10003

CROWN is a trademark of Crown Publishers, Inc.

Manufactured in the United States of America

Library of Congress Cataloging-in-Publication Data
Clayton, Elaine.
Pup in school / written and illustrated by Elaine Clayton.
p. cm.
Summary: Pup stands up to Rodney-dog, the school bully, and
helps him become more friendly and cooperative.
[1. Dogs—Fiction. 2.Bullies—Fiction. 3.Friendship—Fiction. 4.
Schools—Fiction.] ITitle.
PZ7.C57917Pu 1993

ISBN 0-517-59085-9 (trade)
       0-517-59086-7 (lib. bdg.)

10 9 8 7 6 5 4 3 2 1   First Edition

One day, Pup and his friend Pom-Pom decided to construct a restaurant in the Block Corner.

Pup and Pom-Pom had a marvelous time serving
roast blocks glazed with orange gravy, and broiled
blocks with marble peas in butter sauce. All the dogs
in school made reservations to eat at the restaurant.

Then Rodney-dog came to the restaurant. Rodney-dog was quite bossy. He liked to have his way. "Hey, Pup," barked Rodney-dog. "Let me be the chef at this restaurant!"

Pup was too afraid to say no to Rodney-dog.

Later, at Outside Time, Pup and his friends hunted for magic rocks. "Let's look at them with a magnifying glass," said Pup.

Then Rodney-dog appeared. "I want to play!" he demanded.

So Pup asked Rodney-dog, "Would you like to hunt for magic rocks with us?"

But Rodney-dog said, "No. Drop the rocks and come play with me. Now!"

To make matters worse, Rodney-dog wanted to play Karate Frogs. He made Pup be the bad guy. Rodney-dog got to be King Amphibian. He ordered Pup around.

Back in the classroom, when Pup got to read in the Big Chair, Rodney-dog walked up. "I want to sit in the Big Chair. Let *me* sit there!"

Pup was still too afraid to say no, so he let
Rodney-dog have the Big Chair.

After school, Mommy-dog asked, "Did you have a good day, Pup?"
Pup didn't answer.

Mommy-dog looked at Pup. "I know," she said. "How about a movie to cheer us up?"
It was *The Adventures of Boots, the Cowboy Dog*. Pup got some popcorn and a box of Milk-Bones.

Poor Boots! All the other cowboy dogs taunted him. They made him spill his sarsaparilla. They chased him down an alley! They pushed him in the mud!

And they said, "Hey, Boots! You better do what we say!"

But Boots was brave. He said, "I ain't gonna do what you say!"

And the cowboy dogs said, "Oh, yeah?"

And Boots stepped forward and said, "Yeah!"

And then the cowboy dogs stepped back and fell into a water trough!

On the way home from the movie, Pup told Mommy-dog, "I want to be just like Boots. I'm not going to let anyone boss *me* around like those mean cowboy dogs!"

That night, Pup practiced saying "No, Rodney-dog, I won't do what you say" a million times.

He practiced in the mirror.

He practiced at dinner.

He practiced in bed.

The next day was Raggs's birthday. He chose Pup to be first in Doggy, Doggy, Where's Your Bone? But Rodney-dog shouted, "I want to be first!"

Rodney-dog took the bone away from Pup. "Let *me* be first in this game!"

For a moment, Pup was scared.

Then he remembered Boots, and Pup got mad. He took a deep breath and said, "No, Rodney-dog, I *won't* do what you say."

Rodney-dog looked shocked. His nose began to quiver. All of a sudden, he burst into tears.

"No one wants to be my friend!" he cried, then he barked and howled and hid under the table.

Pup stared at Rodney-dog. Now Pup wasn't mad anymore, or scared either. The bad dogs in the movie didn't cry.

"I do want to be your friend, Rodney-dog," Pup said, "but you're always so bossy. You always want to be first in Leap Dog and Red Rover, Red Rover. How would you like it if someone always bossed *you* around?"

Rodney-dog turned away. "Leave me alone," he sniffed. "I don't want any friends anyhow."

For the rest of the week, Pup played with Pom-Pom and Raggs. Pom-Pom let Pup use her sand shovel, and Pup lent Raggs his favorite chew-sock. Pup was having a great time, though he did notice Rodney-dog burying bones all by himself at the other end of the sandbox.

But on Thursday, Rodney-dog gave Pom-Pom the last biscuit at snack time.

And on Friday, he let Raggs go in front of him at the water fountain.

On Monday, Pup was reading in the Big Chair when Rodney-dog came over.

"Here, Pup," he said. "I made this painting for you."

Pup's eyes grew large. "For . . . for me?" he asked. Rodney-dog nodded, and then Pup smiled. "Thanks, Rodney-dog. Would . . . would you like to play Restaurant?" he asked.

Rodney-dog's tail wagged. "I love playing Restaurant!" he said. "I get to be the — I mean, *you* be the chef, Pup!"

"Let's *both* be chefs," said Pup.

And they were.